# MR. NOAH "WHAT'S A QUARANTINE?"

## BY
## CHY HARRIS

NOAH WOKE UP SATURDAY MORNING TO THE SOUND OF THE TV. HE KNEW HIS DAD WAS WATCHING THE NEWS FROM THE SOUND OF IT. HE GOT UP, PUT ON HIS SLIPPERS, AND DRAGGED HIS FEET TO THE BATHROOM.

AS HE CAME OUT THE BATHROOM HIS MOM SAID "DON'T FORGET TO WASH YOUR HANDS!". HE TURNED AROUND AND LISTENED.

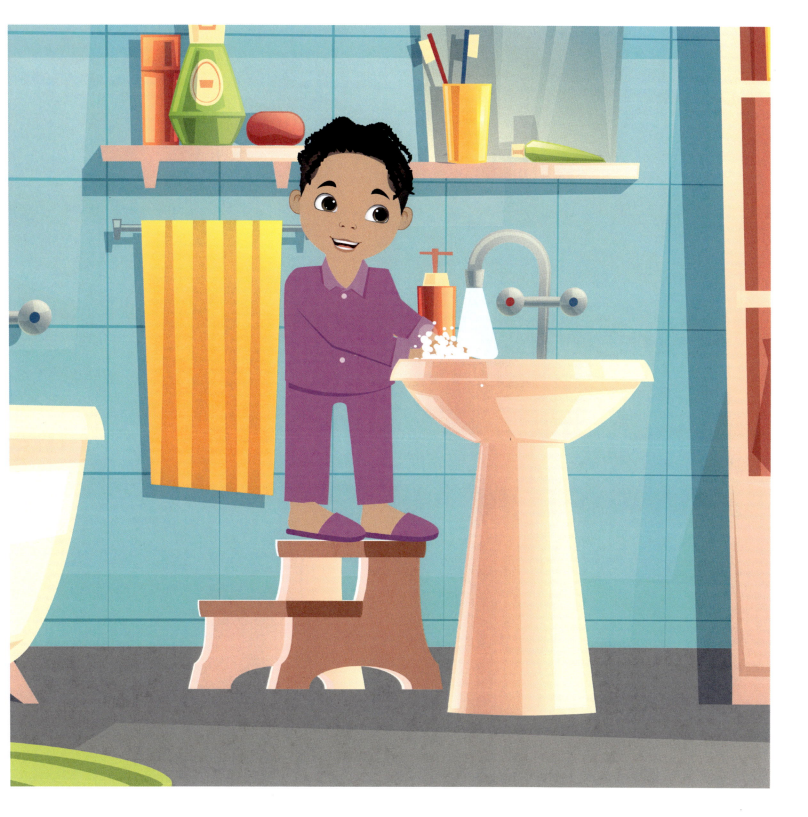

THIS TIME WHEN HE CAME OUT THE BATHROOM HIS MOM SAID " HOLD ON BABY, LET ME TAKE DADDY SOME TEA." "ITS OKAY SON, ENJOY YOUR DAY OFF" DAD SAID AS HE WALKED IN FRONT OF MOM TO THEIR BEDROOM.

That morning Noahs favorite show came on so he went and poured himself some cereal with his favorite bowl and spoon and headed in to the living room. "Table!", mom said as she walked back into the kitchen.

COUGH COUGH! NOAH COULD HEAR DAD IN HIS ROOM COUGHING. HE GOT UP TO GO SEE HIM BUT MOM SAID " DADS NOT FEELING GOOD SO HE'S GOING TO QUARANTINE IN THE ROOM OKAY?". NOAH SAID "WHATS QUARANTINE?"

"IT'S WHEN YOU KEEP YOURSELF AWAY FROM EVERYBODY SO THAT YOU DON'T SPREAD YOUR GERMS TO ANYBODY. DADDY DOESN'T WANT TO GET YOU SICKY". NOAH SAYS "OKAY WELL CAN WE MAKE HIM SOME SOUP?". MOMMY SAYS "THATS A GREAT IDEA!".

NOAH SPENT THE REST OF THE WEEKEND SPENDING TIME WITH HIS MOM AND AUNT AND CHECKING IN ON DAD AND GIVING HIM ALL THE WATER AND SOUP HE COULD EAT AND DRINK.

NOAH WENT TO SCHOOL MONDAY MORNING AND FELT BAD BC DADDY WAS STILL IN THE ROOM. HE DIDN'T EVEN GO TO WORK, OR THE NEXT DAY OR THE NEXT DAY, OR EVEN THE NEXT DAY. NOAH FELT LIKE HE WISH HE WOULD'VE BEEN SICK WITH DADDY TOO. ESPECIALLY WITH ALL THE HOMEWORK HE HAD TO DO THAT WEEK.

FRIDAY MORNING CAME AND NOAH HEARD THE NEWS WHEN HE GOT UP BUT WHEN HE WENT INTO THE LIVING ROOM DADDY WASN'T OUT THERE. HE GOT READY FOR SCHOOL AND MET MOMMY IN THE CAR. AFTER SCHOOL THAT DAY NOAH AND MOMMY WENT TO THE MALL AND EVEN PICKED OUT A NEW HAT FOR DADDY FOR WHEN HE FEELS BETTER.

THEY SHOPPED AND ATE AND NOAH EVEN PLAYED WITH OTHER KIDS AND EVENTUALLY THEY GREW TIRED AND WENT HOME. NOAH RAN DADDY'S FOOD TO THE BASKET ON HIS DOOR AND KNOCKED.

"DAD WE GOT YOUR FAVORITE CHICKEN SANDWICH!, AND I PICKED U OUT A COOKIE TOO!" NOAH SAID. "THANKS BUDDY I BEEN WANTING A COOKIE, NOW GO GET IN THE TUB AND GET READY FOR BED. I LOVE YOU". "LOVE YOU TOO DAD" NOAH SAID AND DID AS HIS FATHER TOLD HIM.

THE NEXT DAY NOAH WOKE UP TO THE SMELL OF PANCAKES. THEY WERE HIS FAVORITE! HE GOT OUT OF BED AND SAID " MOMMMM" ON HIS WAY TO THE KITCHEN.

ONLY TO HIS SURPRISE IT WAS HIS DAD COOKING PANCAKES AND EGGS. NOAH RAN OVER AND HUGGED HIM AROUND THE WAIST. "DAD YOUR NOT IN A QUARANTINE ANYMORE" NOAH SAID.

"NOPE i"M ALL BETTER LiL MAN, AND THANKS FOR KEEPiNG YOUR DiSTANCE AND WASHiNG YOUR HANDS SO THAT YOU DiDN'T GET SiCK."

"IT WAS EASY" NOAH SAID SMILING AT HIS DAD. THEY SHARED PANCAKES AND EGGS AND SUDDENLY NOAH ASKED " WHERE'S MOM?"

COUGH
COUGH